The MAGICAL Underwater ACTIVITY BOOK

By Mia Underwood

Button BOOKS

There is a mysterious, watery world under the sea that is home to incredible creatures and plants. There are creatures so tiny that we can't even see them and some that are HUGE. Amazing eye-popping colors and shapes that are strange and beautiful are all around.

Some of the characters in this book are REAL creatures and others are MAGICAL and can only be seen by very special people. Imagine you could swim, breathe, and live in this watery place. What would it be like?

Draw yourself entering the ocean.
What might you need to take with you?

Welcome to our underwater world

The sea creatures would like to invite you into their magical underwater world. They think you can help them with some very important quests to help save the planet. Are you ready to become an ocean hero?
Let's go!

Some of the sea creatures are missing. Can you add
them to the scene using the stickers found
in the middle of the book?

Microscopic sea creatures
Plankton

Plankton play an important role in life on Earth even though we can barely see them. Being at the very bottom of the marine food chain, they are an essential source of food for larger animals. Phytoplankton (plant plankton) are eaten by zooplankton (animal plankton) and are important for using up carbon dioxide from the atmosphere.

Polychaeta

Anthozoa
(flower animals)

Calycopsis

Eggs

Euphausiidae

Create your own microorganism and give it a name.

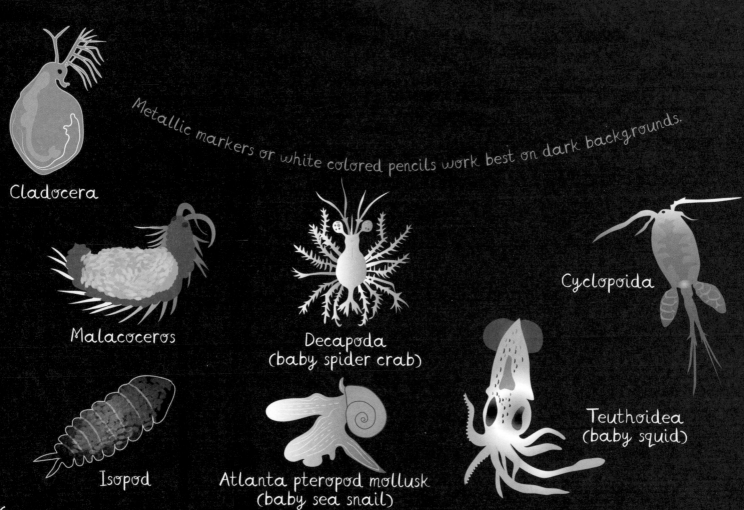

Cladocera

Metallic markers or white colored pencils work best on dark backgrounds.

Malacoceros

Decapoda
(baby spider crab)

Cyclopoida

Isopod

Atlanta pteropod mollusk
(baby sea snail)

Teuthoidea
(baby squid)

Water bears

Also known as tardigrades or moss piglets, these microscopic water dwellers are one of the toughest creatures on planet Earth. They are thought to date back as far as 530 million years and they can still be found today.

Color in the water bear to bring it to life.

They may be tiny, but they make HUGE poops, nearly half the length of their bodies!

FACT
These hardy creatures can survive amazing extremes of heat, pressure, and radiation. They are even able to survive for up to 30 years without food or water. In 2007 some water bears were taken into outer space for 10 days, and even survived exposure to the space vacuum!

Water bears are about 0.01in long, roughly

Paper-fastener
crafty sea creatures

Make your very own magical sea creature, with moveable arms and legs. You could add a stick to the back to transform it into a puppet or attach a loop of string to hang it on your wall.

YOU WILL NEED
----

* Letter or tabloid-sized sheets of card stock
* Scissors
* Tracing paper or a photocopier
* Pencil and pencil sharpener
* Colored markers or pencils
* Paper fasteners (4 per character)
* Strong glue
* Adhesive putty or cork

1. Choose from the opposite page which head, body, arms, legs, fins, tail, or tentacles you would like your creature to have.

2. Trace the body parts onto letter or tabloid-sized card stock (depending how big you want to make your character). Alternatively, photocopy the opposite page and then glue it onto the card stock.

3. Color in the body parts and then cut them out with scissors. Glue the head and tail or tentacles (if you are using them) onto the body and wait for them to dry.

4. Make small holes for the paper fasteners, where shown, on the body, arms, and legs. Ask an adult to help you with this part. Place a piece of adhesive putty or cork on the back of the card stock where you want to make the hole and carefully push the point of a pencil through from the front to the back. Put a paper fastener through the holes to join the arms and legs onto the body, securing at the back by folding out the fasteners.

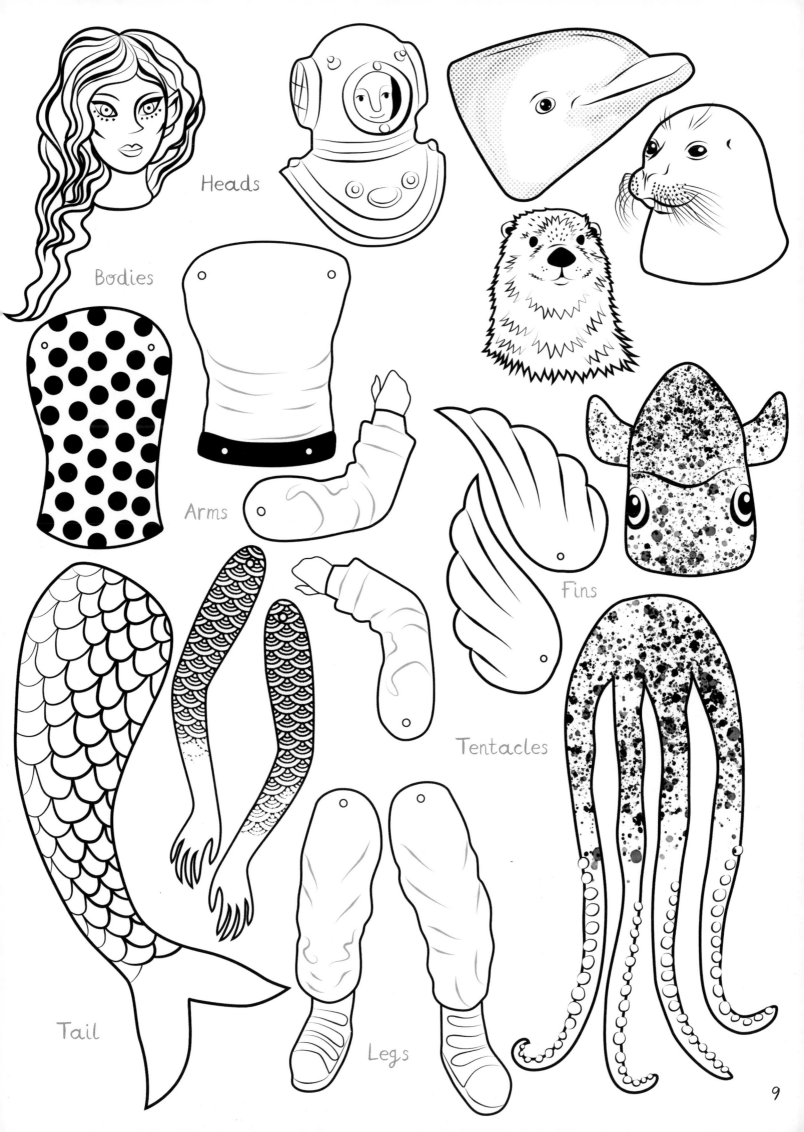

Heads

Bodies

Arms

Fins

Tentacles

Tail

Legs

9

Treasure trails

Can you help the divers find their treasure and get to their goals? Follow the sequence of symbols shown in the key below on the map, drawing a line as you go. Don't draw over the cave walls or the other characters, and watch out for the spiky sea urchins! You can go back the same way if you need to.

Color in all the characters.

Big fish

The world's largest fish is the whale shark, which can grow up to 12 feet long and weighs an average of 14 tons (the same as about three and a half elephants). These friendly giant sharks mainly eat plankton and small fish by filtering water through their enormous mouths while they swim near the surface.

2 points

5 points

10 points

Connect the dotted lines and color in.

Which mouthful contains the most plankton? Use the key opposite to figure out the number value for each symbol. Add them up to see which of the shark's mouthfuls is the biggest.

Secret deep-sea language

Underwater creatures can communicate with each other using sound, light, and vibrations. Some deep-sea creatures, like the angler fish, use bioluminescent light to capture their prey or to create a signal. Humans can use Morse code to send messages with light or sound using dots and dashes to show letters of the alphabet and numbers.

There are three different symbols in Morse code: a short flash of light or noise, usually called a "dit", a long one called a "dah", and a pause. A dah is three times as long as a dit. A pause is the same length as a dit (about one second) between letters, and about three seconds between words.

dit   dah   pause

Morse code

A ·—	B —···	C —·—·	D —··	E ·	F ··—·
G ——·	H ····	I ··	J ·———	K —·—	L ·—··
M ——	N —·	O ———	P ·——·	Q ——·—	R ·—·
S ···	T —	U ··—	V ···—	W ·——	X —··—
Y —·——	Z ——··	0 —————	1 ·————	2 ··———	3 ···——
4 ····—	5 ·····	6 —····	7 ——···	8 ———··	9 ————·

Exchange Morse code messages with a friend

You can send and receive Morse code messages with a friend across a long distance using flashlights. Try to imagine you are deep-sea creatures communicating with each other. This is a fun activity to do outdoors, when it is dark. You could also try this with something that makes a beeping noise.

YOU WILL NEED

* 2 x photocopies of the Morse code (on the opposite page)
* 2 x flashlights to create light signals (or something that "beeps" for sound)
* 2 x pieces of paper and pencils

1. Create a conversation by taking it in turns to send and receive messages using the flashlights to create bursts of light.

2. Write down on the piece of paper the dits, dahs, and pauses you receive and then translate them afterward using your copy of the Morse code. Your messages could give locations for a hidden treat.

There are hidden messages in the book you can decode (see pages 21 and 29).

FACT

Morse code is named after Samuel Morse, who helped invent it to use on an electric telegraph machine. It was used for secret messages during World War I and World War II but it is not used as much today as new technology has gradually replaced it.

Message in a bottle

The mermaid has discovered an old glass bottle on the sea bed with a mysterious map inside. An important piece of the map is missing, which shows where to find a lost treasure chest. Can you help her find it? Go to the middle of the book to find the sticker that fits into the map.

Draw and color in the missing parts of these sea creatures to make them come to life.

Fill in the missing map grid references below. The first one has been done for you.

GOLD SKULL: C6

LAVA WITH HEALING POWERS:

TREASURE CHEST (FIND THE STICKER):

Go to the middle of the book to find the sticker that fits this missing piece of the map.

THE LOST SEA

8 7 6 5 4 3 2 1

A B C D E F G H

Shipwreck

The mermaid and her friends have found the shipwreck and the treasure chest using the mysterious map. The ocean has its own store of natural treasures, too. How many hidden pearls can you find? Watch out for the great white sharks!

Color in the mermaid and her best friend

MMEARDI — - - - - - - -
UOCOPST — - - - - - - -
CKSIPWHRE — - - - - - - - - -
PERSAL — - - - - - -
ERRTAUSE — - - - - - - -
RASKH — - - - - -
LWCON SIFH — - - - - - - - -
ROCLA — - - - - -
EWASEDE — - - - - - - -

Unscramble these words to unlock the treasure chest. The answers can all be seen in the picture.

The MAGICAL underwater SEA HOUSE

Add some magical sea creatures and shell ornaments to these empty underwater rooms using the stickers found in the middle of the book.

Decode the
secret message
using the key
on page 14.

Design and draw your own
UNDERWATER HOME

You can also use any spare stickers from the middle of the book.

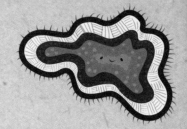

Micro sea beasts

Stare at the shapes for a while, then draw the sea
creature that you see appearing before your eyes.
Some have been done for you.

A — Z

Find at least one sea creature in the picture for each letter of the alphabet. Can you spot them all? Check off each letter as you match it up to a creature.

Box jellyfish

Hammerhead shark

CAN YOU FIND 30 ANCHOVIES?

Walrus

Penguin

Ray

Jellyfish

Zebra shark

Grouper

Otter

Sea snake

Unicorn fish

Viperfish

Seagrass

Eel

xiphodorsal

Isopod

Killer whale

Dolphin

Narwhal

Anchovies

Moonfish

Turtle

Flounder

Yellow tang

X-ray fish

Lionfish

Angel fish

Sea horse

Clown fish

Barnacles

Krill

Coral

Queen conch

Crab

Sea urchins

Starfish

A B C D E F G H I J K L M N O P Q R S T U V W X Y Z

Ocean cleanup

The sea creatures' home is littered with plastic trash and needs a massive cleanup. Can you help by counting all the plastic objects so they can be gathered up?

OH NO! This could be a plastic straw you used from a few years ago floating in the ocean somewhere!

How many of each plastic item can you spot?

TOOHBRUSHES ◯   BAGS ◯   BOTTLE TOPS ◯

STRAWS ◯   FORKS ◯   KNIVES ◯

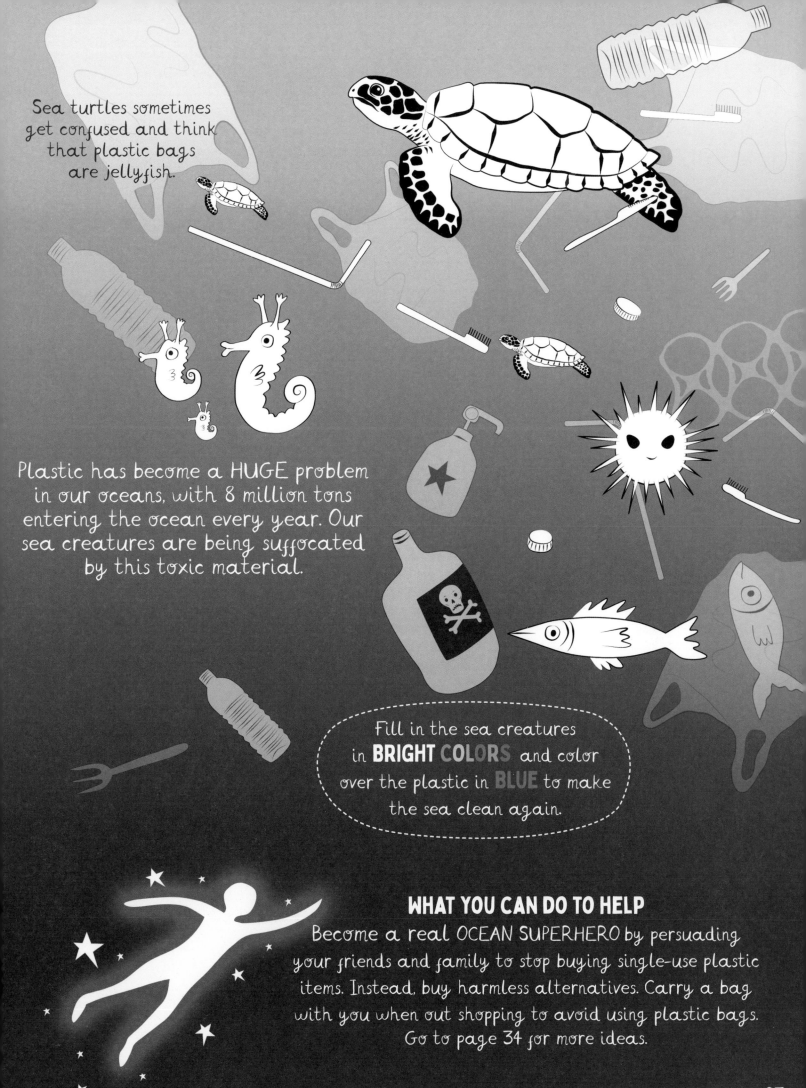

Sea turtles sometimes get confused and think that plastic bags are jellyfish.

Plastic has become a HUGE problem in our oceans, with 8 million tons entering the ocean every year. Our sea creatures are being suffocated by this toxic material.

Fill in the sea creatures in **BRIGHT COLORS** and color over the plastic in **BLUE** to make the sea clean again.

WHAT YOU CAN DO TO HELP

Become a real OCEAN SUPERHERO by persuading your friends and family to stop buying single-use plastic items. Instead, buy harmless alternatives. Carry a bag with you when out shopping to avoid using plastic bags. Go to page 34 for more ideas.

Plastic invasion

FACT
Microplastics are tiny fragments of plastic that are so small they cannot be seen with the naked eye. They have been found at the very bottom of our oceans and many sea creatures are eating them. Harmful chemicals can make the creatures sick and the tiny plastic pieces end up in our food chain and water supplies.

Microplastics can build up inside the tummies of our sea creatures making them very sick.

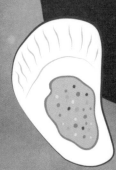

Shellfish are able to filter out microplastics from the ocean.

Microorganisms, like plankton, eat microplastics as they think they are food but they can get sick and die.

Microplastics could even end up on your plate for dinner... yuck!

Decode the secret message using the key on page 14.

Color in the scene.

The blue whale
The largest animal in the world

When the blue whale surfaces, it exhales through the blowhole at the top of its body sending a cloud of pressurized air as high as 30 feet upward!

Size compared to an average adult human.

CAN YOU MATCH UP the blue whale's favorite sea creatures to their silhouettes? Draw a line to link each pair back together.

FACTS

The blue whale is the largest animal that has ever lived and can grow up to 100 feet long. There were many blue whales in nearly all our oceans until they were hunted almost to extinction by whalers in the twentieth century. Blue whales are also the loudest animal in the world, their call can be up to 188 decibels! This loud sound can be heard at very long distances underwater.

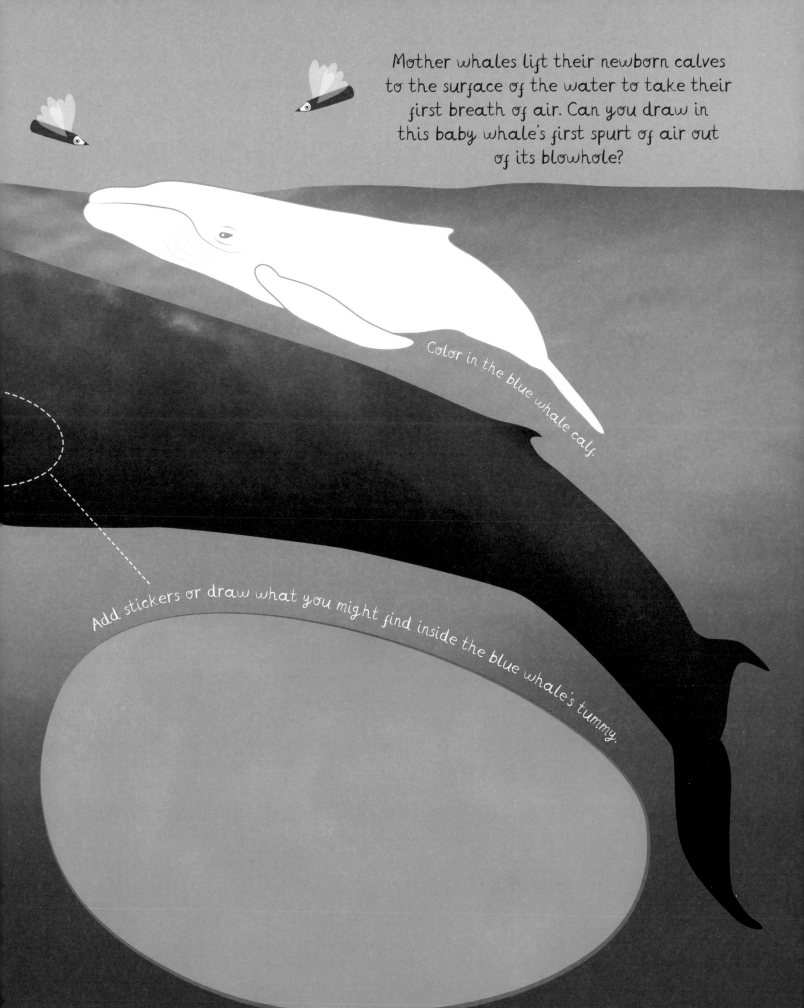

Mother whales lift their newborn calves to the surface of the water to take their first breath of air. Can you draw in this baby whale's first spurt of air out of its blowhole?

Color in the blue whale calf.

Add stickers or draw what you might find inside the blue whale's tummy.

The blue whale's favorite foods are krill, plankton, and small fish. They eat about 4 tons of food every day, which is about 40 million krill.

Color in the sea otters

Did you know that underneath a sea otter's forearm is a pouch to store their favorite rock to crack open shells and sea urchins?

Welcome to our underwater world, pages 4-5

Treasure map, page 17

View from inside your DEEP-SEA submarine, pages 52-53

The magical underwater sea house, pages 20-21

Make your very own deep-sea submarine, pages 48-49

Real or made-up?, pages 58-59

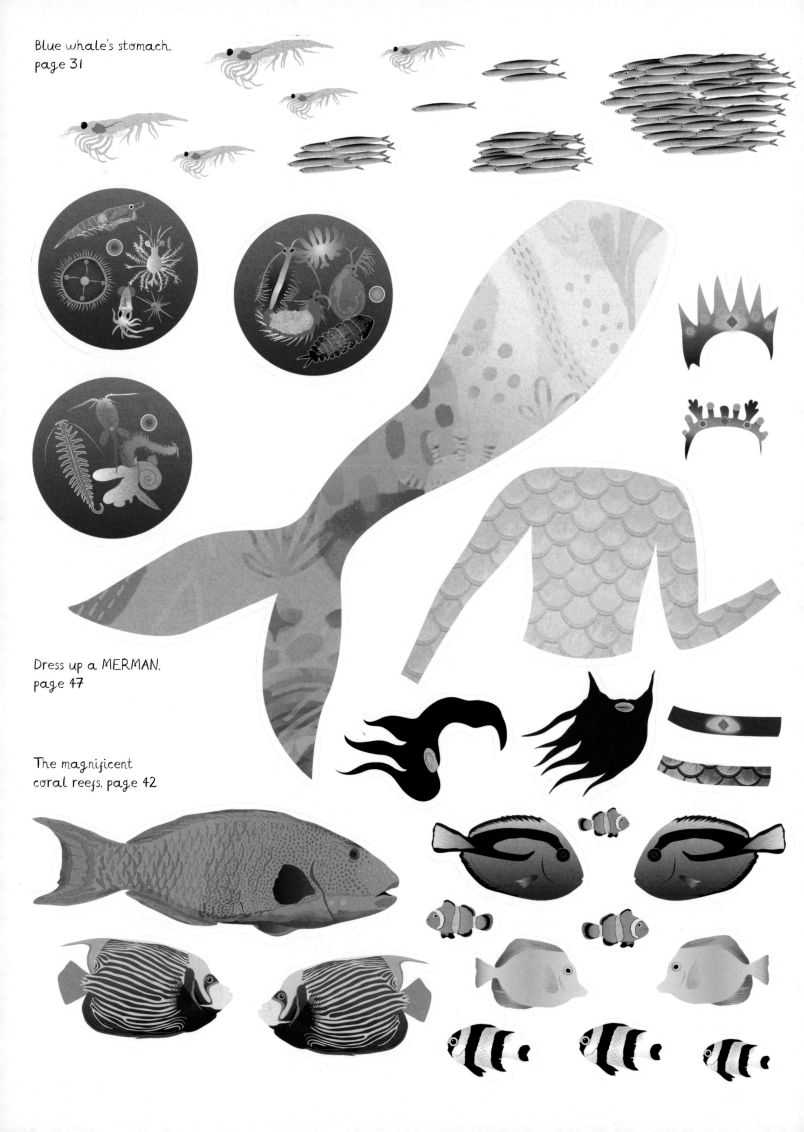

Blue whale's stomach,
page 31

Dress up a MERMAN,
page 47

The magnificent
coral reefs, page 42

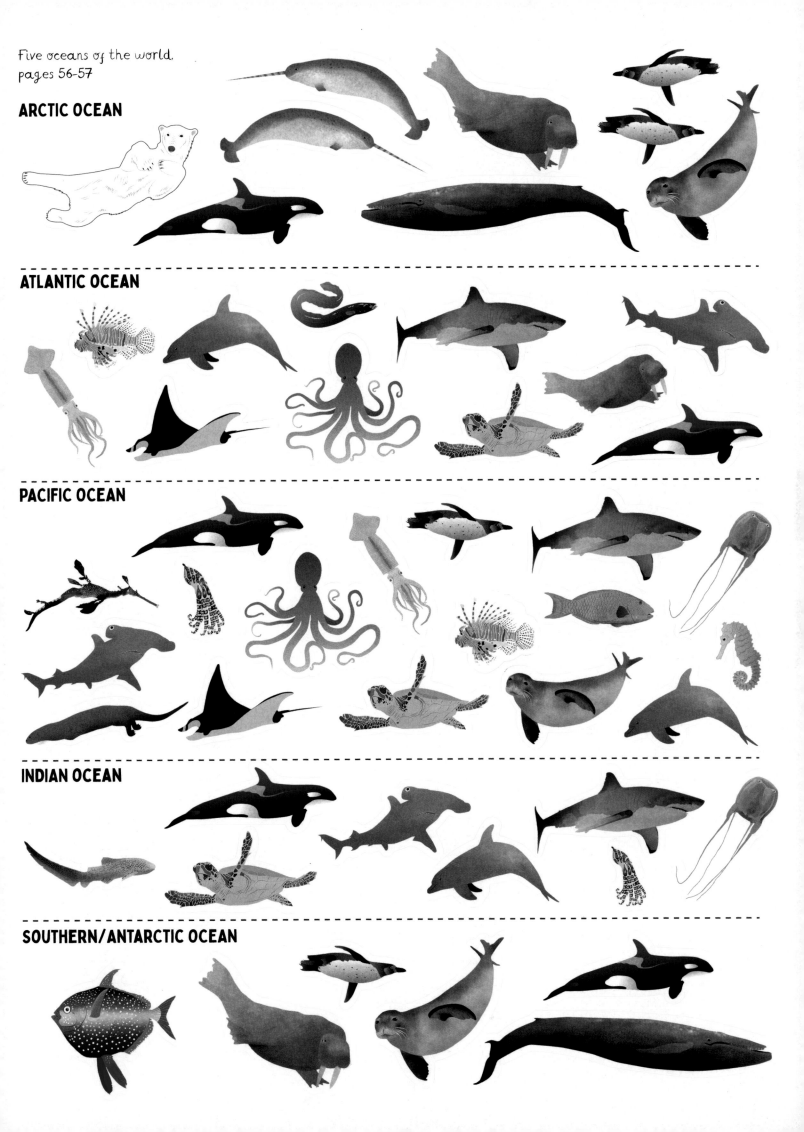

Five oceans of the world,
pages 56-57

ARCTIC OCEAN

ATLANTIC OCEAN

PACIFIC OCEAN

INDIAN OCEAN

SOUTHERN/ANTARCTIC OCEAN

Seaweed sushi

VEGGIE MAKI ROLLS

YOU WILL NEED

- 1 x packet of nori (sheets of dried seaweed)
- 50oz sushi rice
- 1 teaspoon of sugar (optional)
- 2 tablespoons of Japanese rice vinegar
- ½ a cucumber, cut into thin strips
  (you could also use carrot or avocado)
- Large spoon
- Serrated knife
- Sushi rolling mat (makisu)
- Small bowl of water

1. Cook the sushi rice following the instructions on the package. Once cooked, add the sugar and vinegar to the rice and stir in while it is still hot. Allow the rice to cool.

2. Lay a sheet of nori on the rolling mat with the rough side facing upward, and the lines in the nori running vertically. Take a few spoonfuls of the cooled-down rice and spread it out evenly over the nori sheet, leaving an empty strip along the top.

3. Lay a couple of cucumber strips in a row across the center of the rice.

4. Wet your fingers in the water and dab across the top edge of the nori to help it stick. With the help of your mat, start rolling from the bottom, applying a bit of pressure as you go. Roll all the way up to the top, making sure the strip with the water on has sealed and stuck to hold the roll together. Remove the mat to reveal your maki roll.

5. With the help of an adult, dip the end of a serrated knife in water and cut the maki roll in half, trim off the uneven ends and slice the maki into six even pieces.

Ball of rice with cut-out seaweed shapes on top

Broccoli and cherry tomatoes

HELLO

You can cut out shapes or letters from a sheet of nori with scissors to create a fun lunch box treat.

Become a real
OCEAN SUPERHERO

Design your
OCEAN SUPERHERO
costume

THINGS YOU CAN DO TO HELP OUR PLANET

- Take a reusable water bottle and shopping bag when you go out.
- Walk, scoot, or cycle to school instead of being driven in a car.
- When choosing presents for other people, look for something plastic-free.
- When writing a present wishlist, try to choose fewer plastic objects.
- If you live near the ocean, organize a beach-cleaning event with friends and family.
- Ask your school about running a plastic-free fair to help teach other kids and adults.

Design an ocean-cleaning gadget
Can you invent a gadget that can clean up plastic from the ocean?

How will it collect LARGE floating plastic items?
How will it collect tiny microplastics?
How will it detect what is and what isn't made of plastic?

Complete all the problems to stop the sea creatures from getting stuck in the fishing nets.

×3

3

9   10   1

8   2

×3   3

7   3

6   5   4

Look at the instruction in the middle of the fishing net and work around in a circle doing each problem. One has been done for you in each net.

÷2

2   4

20

18   6

÷2

16   8

14 12 10

6

+6

15

10   1

9   2

8   +6   3

7   3

6   5   4

Why did the octopus blush?
Because it saw the bottom of the ocean.

Complete the number sequences in the octopus's arms to set her free from the fishing net.

OCTOPUS Math

How many arms does an octopus have?

Create your very own sea creature
CHARACTER
for a story

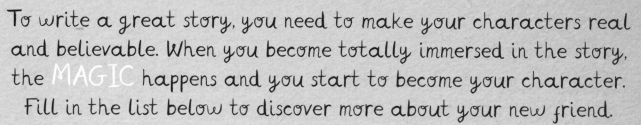

To write a great story, you need to make your characters real and believable. When you become totally immersed in the story, the MAGIC happens and you start to become your character. Fill in the list below to discover more about your new friend.

YOUR CHARACTER'S NAME: ....

KEY CHARACTERISTICS

> Female/male/other? ....

> How old is it? ....

> What does it like to eat? ....

> How big/tall/small is it? ....

> How is it feeling? (e.g. happy, sad, hungry) ....

> What is its goal? ....

> Where does it live? ....

> What is its voice like? (try sounding it out loud) ....

> Who else is in its family? ....

> What is it good at? ....

> What is its favorite color? ....

> Does it have a magical power? ....

> Who is its best friend? ....

> How does it look? (e.g. scaly, silky, spiky) ....

Draw your sea creature here

USE YOUR IMAGINATION

ROLL A STORY

Roll a dice once for each of the categories in the table, picking the plot detail with the same number. Use your imagination to fill in the rest of the story on the opposite page, giving it a beginning, middle, and end.

DICE NUMBER	CHARACTER YOU MEET	PLACE	ACTION	PROBLEM
⚀	Blue whale	A coral reef	Grows bioluminescent antennae	Gets sucked into a whirlpool
⚁	Mermaid	Under an iceberg	Swims superfast	Needs to find a lost key
⚂	Moray eel	Underwater cave	Squirts ink	Gets caught in a fishing net
⚃	Great white shark	In a shipwreck	Has a tea party with a mermaid	Finds a locked treasure box
⚄	Giant octopus	At the bottom of the ocean	Rescues a blue whale calf	Gets lost in the dark depths of the ocean
⚅	Baby seal	In a submarine	Fights a sea monster	Gets trapped in a whale's tummy

WRITE DOWN YOUR STORY

Your main character from pages 38-39:

Character you meet:

Place:

Action:

Problem:

You create the solution/end:

TITLE: _____

BEGINNING:

MIDDLE:

END:

THE MAGNIFICENT
Coral reefs

Can you find your way through the maze on the sea turtle's shell?

START

FINISH

FACT

Half of the world's coral reefs have died due to climate change and the rising temperatures in our oceans. When the ocean gets too warm, corals lose the colored, microscopic algae living in their tissue, which provide them with food. When corals are without the algae for too long, they die of starvation. Coral reefs provide vital food and shelter for marine life that feeds millions of people. If we lose our magical coral-reef ecosystems it will be a very serious disaster.

Be an OCEAN HERO and color the coral reef on this side to bring it back to life. Then, use the stickers from the middle of the book to add the fish back in.

Venomous sea creatures

CAN YOU HELP TWIGGY
get to her friend Mouser on the other side of the venomous sea creatures, without getting stung? Draw a line without going over the words or pictures.

BOX JELLYFISH
Usually found in Australia, these creatures are so venomous they can kill a human within two minutes.

Twiggy

STINGRAYS
Stingrays have several sharp and venomous barbs on their tails that they use when they feel threatened. It is very rare for them to attack humans unless provoked.

FACT
Recent studies show that venomous sea creatures are on the rise due to climate change. Warming oceans could welcome in a whole new army of dangerous creatures, from sea snakes to jellyfish and lionfish.

BLUE-RINGED OCTOPUS
The blue-ringed octopus is small but carries enough venom to kill 26 adult humans within minutes. Their bites are tiny and often painless, so many victims do not realize they have been bitten.

SEA SNAKES

The beaked sea snake can kill about eight people with just three drops of venom! Fortunately, it is very rare for humans to be bitten, unless they provoke the snake.

Mouser

WHICH TWO PUFFER FISH ARE IDENTICAL?

When you have figured it out, color them all in.

PUFFER FISH

These cute but deadly creatures puff up when they are in danger. Their spikes contain enough venom to kill 30 adult humans or animals...yikes!

LIONFISH

Lionfish are highly venomous: they can inject neurotoxins from spines on their fins. As lionfish populations continue to increase, so does the likelihood of human injuries.

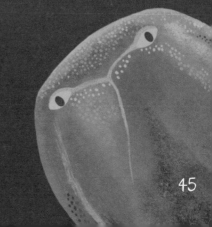

1. First draw the head and neck.

2. Add the top half of the body, choosing whether you'd prefer the arms to be up or down.

3. Add the mermaid's swishy tail.

How to draw a
MERMAID

4. When you are happy with your outline, add the flowing hair, facial details, and the scales on her tail. Your drawing is now ready to color in.

You could also trace this mermaid using tracing paper and a pencil, or photocopy it.

Dress up a
MERMAN

Use the stickers from the
middle of the book to
DRESS UP the merman

CRAFT

Make your very own
DEEP-SEA SUBMARINE

Here is a great way to reuse cardboard boxes and packaging. You will need an adult to help cut out all the pieces. The technique for this project uses a slotting mechanism.

YOU WILL NEED

- 2 x tabloid sheets of corrugated cardboard
- Photocopy of the templates opposite (enlarge them to 200%)
- Pencil and tracing paper
- Knife or sharp scissors
- Paint or colored markers
- Glue

STEP 1

Enlarge the templates opposite on a photocopier to 200%. Trace them with tracing paper and a pencil and then transfer them onto the cardboard. Cut out the right number of all the pieces.

STEP 2

Slot together 2 x A and 2 x B pieces, (shape B at the front and back). This is where the deep-sea explorers sit. You can draw the people on the front and draw on the inside what they might take with them.

STEP 3

Now slot the shape you made in STEP 2 into shape D. Slot shape E at the front end of shape D.

STEP 4

Next put one shape C on top of the A and B shape to give it a roof (you can still peek inside). Put one shape C on the bottom to give it a base.

STEP 5

Glue shape G onto shape F and then onto the roof for decoration. Now your submarine is ready to paint. You can also add the stickers found in the middle of the book, once it is dry.

48

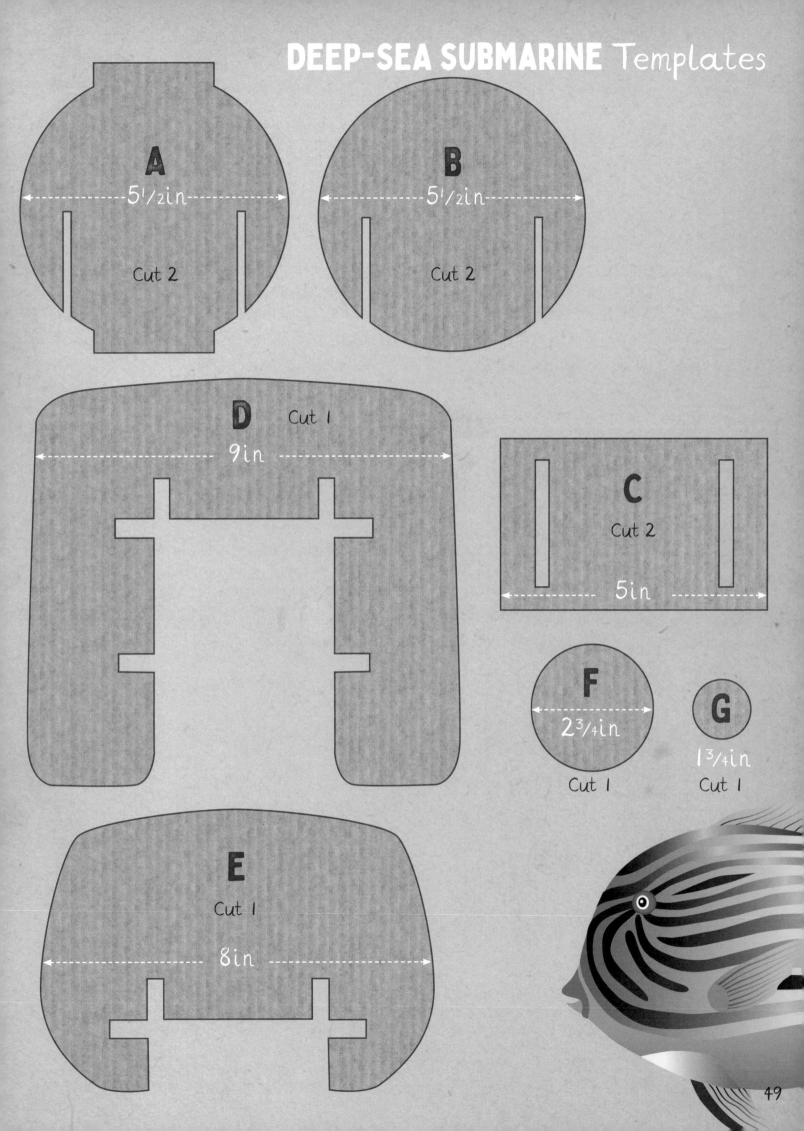

DEEP-SEA SUBMARINE Templates

A
5¹/₂in
Cut 2

B
5¹/₂in
Cut 2

D Cut 1
9in

C
Cut 2
5in

F
2³/₄in
Cut 1

G
1³/₄in
Cut 1

E
Cut 1
8in

How DEEP is the ocean?

Draw your submarine going to the deepest place in all the oceans.
The Mariana Trench is 7 miles deep in the Pacific Ocean.
You can find out where it is on the map on page 56.

It would take 785 buses lined up to reach the bottom of the Mariana Trench!

Only three subs have made it
to the deepest place on Earth,
most recently in early 2019.

FACT
Deep-sea
explorers have
discovered plastic
bags and microplastics
on the ocean floor
of the Mariana
Trench.

PLASTIC ISLAND

CONNECT THE DOTS
Create GERTRUDE, a magical, plastic-eating machine to gobble up ALL the MESS. You can invent your own ocean-cleaning gadget on page 35.

FACT
There is a real plastic island about 656,000 square miles in size. That is about seven times the size of the United Kingdom. It is the largest in the world and is located between Hawaii and California. You can find it on page 56 and you'll be surprised to see how big it really is...
YUCK!

GHOST NETS
Most of the plastic in our oceans is old fishing nets. They are a danger to marine habitats and sea life.

VIEW FROM INSIDE YOUR
DEEP-SEA
SUBMARINE

Add stickers from the middle of the book to complete the view from your submarine.

Can you help find the words in the word search to complete the DEEP-SEA quest?

ANGLER FISH
DARK
DEEP
OCTOPUS
SEA
SQUID
SUBMARINE
VIPERFISH

A	N	G	L	E	R	F	I	S	H
S	M	E	A	U	G	R	O	K	V
W	U	E	D	Y	V	C	J	R	I
M	S	B	L	U	T	H	N	A	P
E	D	W	M	O	P	E	J	D	E
L	M	E	P	A	G	E	J	C	R
D	I	U	Q	S	R	I	E	Z	F
W	S	Y	U	O	J	I	L	D	I
I	G	U	U	X	C	C	N	X	S
S	J	G	S	O	E	C	O	E	H

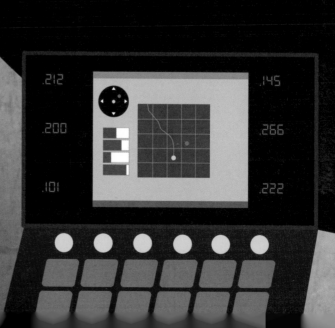

What supplies would you take with you for your DEEP-SEA voyage? Draw them on the shelves.

.212

.200

.101

.145

.206

.222

SPOT THE DIFFERENCE
Can you spot five differences between the left and right control panels?

TROPICAL

The Pacific and Indian oceans
have warm seas where these
creatures thrive.

Color in all the different
sea creatures.

COLD

The cold Arctic and Antarctic oceans are home to many different creatures.

Climate change is causing the polar ice caps to melt.

How many penguins can you spot?

Five oceans of the world

Look at the stickers in the middle of
the book and add the sea creatures
to the oceans that they live in.

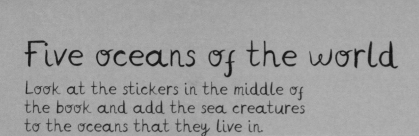

ARCTIC OCEAN

North
America

THE FLOATING
PLASTIC ISLAND
(growing every day)

**ATLANTIC
OCEAN**

Africa

PACIFIC OCEAN

South
America

SOUTHERN/ANTARCTIC OCEAN

Antarctica

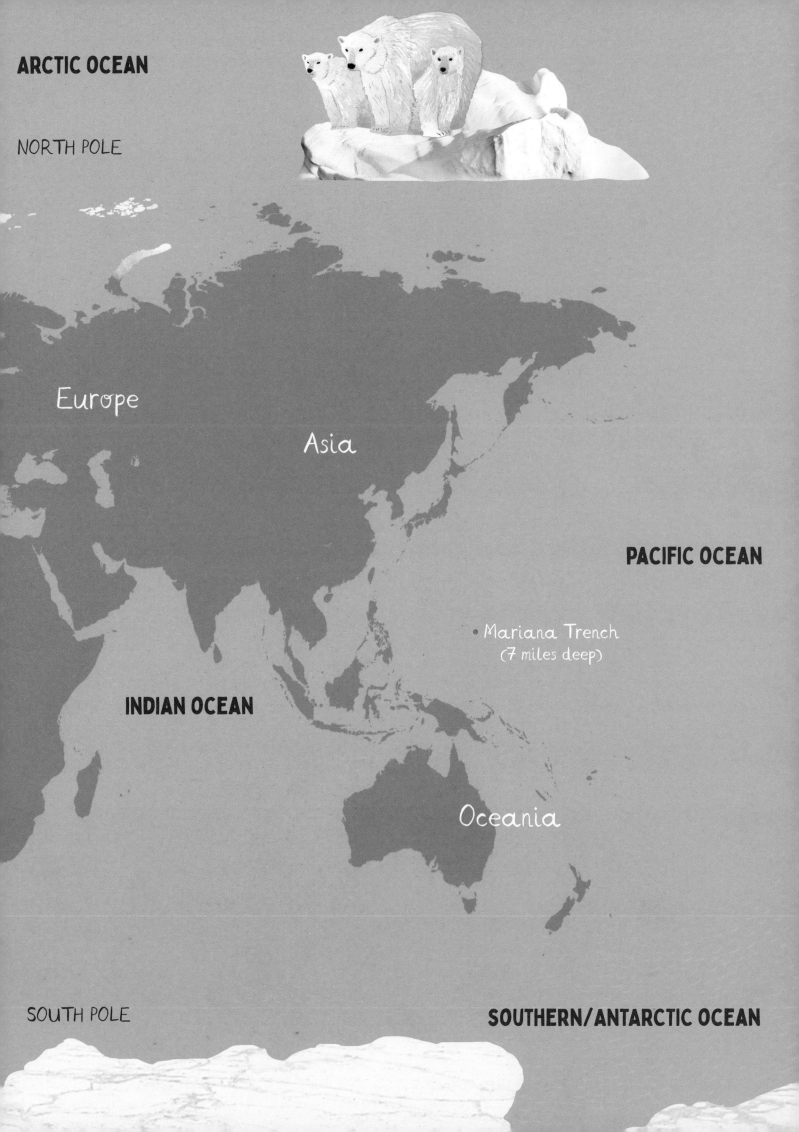

ARCTIC OCEAN

NORTH POLE

Europe

Asia

PACIFIC OCEAN

• Mariana Trench
(7 miles deep)

INDIAN OCEAN

Oceania

SOUTH POLE

SOUTHERN/ANTARCTIC OCEAN

What lives down there?
REAL OR MADE-UP?

Use the stickers to mark the sea creatures on these pages with a check or an X to say whether they are real or made-up, then check the answers on the last page.

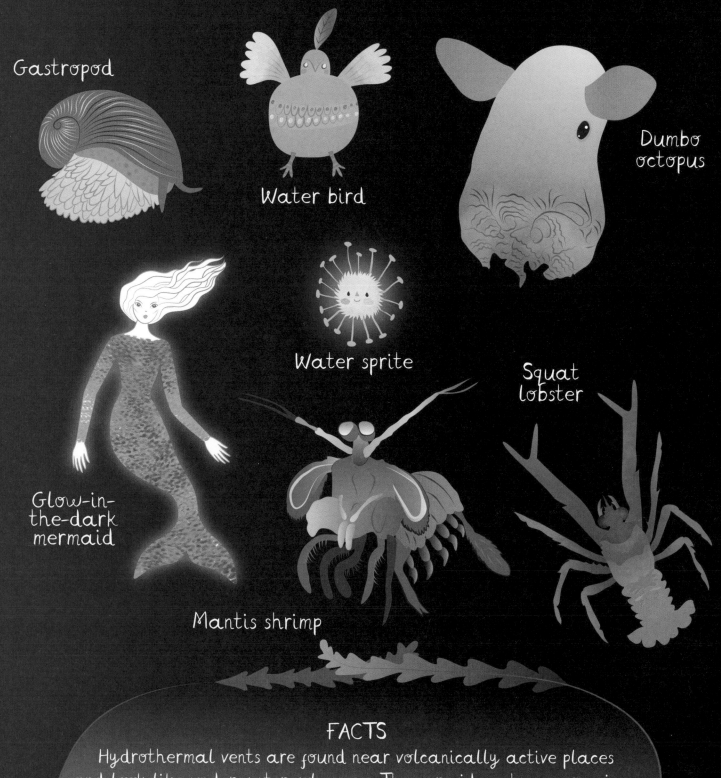

Gastropod

Water bird

Dumbo octopus

Glow-in-the-dark mermaid

Water sprite

Squat lobster

Mantis shrimp

FACTS
Hydrothermal vents are found near volcanically active places and look like underwater volcanoes. They provide a home for unique ecosystems and organisms in the deep ocean. More than 590 animal species have been discovered living near these vents, and these species vary within the five different oceans.

HYDROTHERMAL VENTS

These are chimney-like formations that come out of the ocean floor, spewing out jets of sulfur. Thanks to these vents, life thrives in the deepest parts of the oceans, where sunlight cannot reach and the seawater is extremely cold.

Jewel jellyfish

Micro human

Water bear

Giant tube worm

Blooper fish

Copepod

Giant spider crab

Zoarcid fish

Giant clam

Sea monsters

DEEP, DEEP down in the darkness, you are surrounded by strange creatures who would love to meet you. This sea monster is called Steve. He is about the size of a house, so don't get too close since he is a bit snappy. Color him in to make him come to life...if you dare!

What do you think Steve might say to you?

And, what would you reply?

Steve is actually very lonely since he lives at the bottom of the sea where it is very dark. Can you draw him some friends? Metallic markers or white colored pencils work best on dark backgrounds.

Spot the difference
Can you find eleven differences between these two underwater creatures?

Which two micro beasts are exactly the same?

REAL DEEP-SEA CREATURES

ANGLER FISH

These strange fish live in the Atlantic and Antarctic oceans. They have a lure at the top of their head, which glows to attract their prey.

VAMPIRE SQUID

They look like they fly through the water when they start flapping their fins. Vampire squids can reach the speed of two body lengths per second.

GULPER EEL

A deep-sea fish rarely seen by humans, though sometimes caught in fishing nets. Its enormous mouth is much larger than its body. The mouth is loosely hinged, and can be opened wide enough to swallow an animal much larger than itself.

NAUTILUS

The nautilus can be found in tropical waters in the Indian Ocean and around southern Japan and Australia. It usually lives at depths of 165 to 1,900 feet below the surface.

VIPERFISH

This is a fierce predator. It flashes light from the sides of its body and has a lure to attract prey or a mate.

GIANT ISOPOD

This is an important scavenger on the ocean floor. The deeper an isopod lives, the bigger it gets.

DUMBO OCTOPUS

The cutest octopus in the world gets its name from its big ears. They can grow over 5 feet long and can change color.

COLOR IN
the deep-sea creatures using the
opposite page as your guide.

Answers

Pages 12–13: top left mouthful 34, top right 21, bottom left (biggest) 50, bottom right 29. Page 17: Lava = F7, Treasure chest (found on the sticker) = E3. Pages 18–19: hidden pearls = 18; unscrambled words = mermaid, octopus, shipwreck, pearls, treasure, shark, clown fish, coral, seaweed. Page 21: secret message = Welcome, choose a room to live in. Pages 24–25: A = anchovies, angel fish; B = barnacles, box jellyfish; C = clown fish, coral, crab; D = dolphin; E = eel, F = flounder; G = grouper; H = hammerhead shark; I = isopod; J = jellyfish; K = killer whale, krill; L = lionfish; M = moonfish; N = narwhal; O = otter; P = penguin; Q = queen conch; R = ray; S = seagrass, sea horse, sea snake, sea urchins, starfish; T = turtle; U = unicorn fish; V = viperfish; W = walrus; X = xiphodorsal, x-ray fish; Y = yellow tang; Z = zebra shark. Pages 26–27: plastic objects = 39; 4 toothbrushes, 6 bags, 4 bottle tops, 7 straws, 3 forks, 3 knives. Page 29: secret message = Please help us clean the ocean on page 35. Page 36: (clockwise from given answer) top web = 6, 9, 12, 15, 18, 21, 24, 27, 30; middle web = 7, 8, 9, 10, 1, 2, 3, 4, 5; bottom web = 16, 7, 8, 9, 10, 11, 12, 13, 14. Page 37: number sequences in the octopus legs clockwise starting from top right: 8, 16, 24, 32, 40, 48, 56, 64, 72, 80, 88, 96, 104, 112, 120; 7, 14, 21, 28, 35, 42, 49, 56, 63, 70, 77, 84, 91, 98, 105; 6, 12, 18, 24, 30, 36, 42, 48, 54, 60, 66, 72, 78, 84, 90, 96, 102, 108; 5, 10, 15, 20, 25, 30, 35, 40, 45, 50, 55, 60, 65, 70, 75, 80, 85, 90; 4, 8, 12, 16, 20, 24, 28, 32, 36, 40, 44, 48, 52, 56, 60, 64; 3, 6, 9, 12, 15, 18, 21, 24, 27, 30, 33, 36, 39, 42, 45, 48, 51; 2, 4, 6, 8, 10, 12, 14, 16, 18, 20, 22, 24, 26, 28; 1, 2, 3, 4, 5, 6, 7, 8, 9, 10, 11, 12, 13; an octopus has 8 arms. Page 45: (clockwise from top) 3rd and 5th puffer fish are identical. Page 55: 21 penguins. Pages 58–59: real = gastropods, dumbo octopus, mantis shrimp, squat lobster, water bear, copepod, giant tube worm, giant spider crab, zoarcid fish, giant clam; made-up = water bird, glow-in-the-dark mermaid, jewel jellyfish, micro human, blooper fish, water sprite. Page 61: (clockwise from top) 1st and 4th micro beasts are identical.

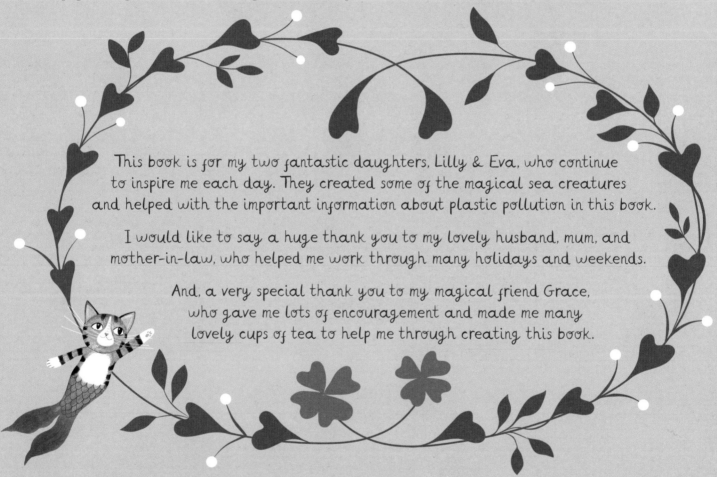

This book is for my two fantastic daughters, Lilly & Eva, who continue to inspire me each day. They created some of the magical sea creatures and helped with the important information about plastic pollution in this book.

I would like to say a huge thank you to my lovely husband, mum, and mother-in-law, who helped me work through many holidays and weekends.

And, a very special thank you to my magical friend Grace, who gave me lots of encouragement and made me many lovely cups of tea to help me through creating this book.

First published 2020 by Button Books, an imprint of Guild of Master Craftsman Publications Ltd Castle Place, 166 High Street, Lewes, East Sussex BN7 1XU.
Text © Mia Underwood, 2020. Copyright in the Work © GMC Publications Ltd, 2020. Illustrations © Mia Underwood, 2020. ISBN 978 1 78708 045 4. Distributed by Publishers Group West in the United States. All rights reserved. The right of Mia Underwood to be identified as the author of this work has been asserted in accordance with the Copyright, Designs, and Patents Act 1988, sections 77 and 78. No part of this publication may be reproduced, stored in a retrieval system, or transmitted in any form or by any means without the prior permission of the publisher and copyright owner. This book is sold subject to the condition that all designs are copyright and are not for commercial reproduction without the permission of the designer and copyright owner. While every effort has been made to obtain permission from the copyright holders for all material used in this book, the publishers will be pleased to hear from anyone who has not been appropriately acknowledged and to make the correction in future reprints. The publishers and author can accept no legal responsibility for any consequences arising from the application of information, advice, or instructions given in this publication. A catalog record for this book is available from the British Library.
Publisher: Jonathan Bailey; Production Manager: Jim Bulley, Jo Pallett; Senior Project Editor: Virginia Brehaut; Managing Art Editor: Gilda Pacitti. Color origination by GMC Reprographics. Printed and bound in China. Warning! Choking Hazard—small parts. Not suitable for children under 3 years.

For more information on Button Books, contact:
GMC Publications Ltd Castle Place, 166 High Street, Lewes, East Sussex, BN7 1XU, United Kingdom
Tel: +44 (0)1273 488005   www.buttonbooks.co.uk